The Secret Keeper

Anna Grossnickle Hines

JUL   1991

 Greenwillow Books, New York

Watercolor paints and colored pencils were used for the full-color art.
The text type is ITC Usherwood.

Printed in Hong Kong by South China Printing Company (1988) Ltd.
First Edition   10 9 8 7 6 5 4 3 2 1

Library of Congress Cataloging-in-Publication Data
Hines, Anna Grossnickle.
The secret keeper/Anna Grossnickle Hines
p.   cm.
Summary: Unhappy to be the only one in his house without
Christmas secrets, Joshua is relieved when Grandma
comes and helps him have some secrets of his own.
ISBN 0-688-08945-3.   ISBN 0-688-08946-1 (lib bdg.)
[1. Secrets—Fiction. 2. Christmas—Fiction.
3. Family life—Fiction.]   I. Title PZ7.H572Se 1990
[E]—dc 20   89-34618   CIP   AC

For Evan,

who also makes books

Our house was full of secrets. The garage was locked up tight. A sign on the door said, "Keep out. Santa's Workshop, South Annex." Penny helped me read it.

"Why can't I go in there?" I asked.

"Christmas secrets, Joshua," Daddy called from behind the door.

Mother was sewing in the bedroom. I could hear her sewing machine through the door, but it was locked, too. "I have to tell her something," I said. "You can't," said Abby. "Christmas secrets."

Penny and Abby were whispering. "What are we going to give Mother and Daddy for Christmas?" asked Abby.

"Shhh!" said Penny, pointing her thumb at me.

"I want to give them a present, too," I said. "I won't tell."

"Oh, ha!" said Abby.

"You might not mean to, Joshie," said Penny. "But you might forget."

Grandma came to stay for the holidays. She
sleeps in my room. She put a bag in the closet.

"What's in there?" I asked.

"Christmas secrets," Grandma said.

"I hate Christmas," I said.

"There are too
many secrets."

"What you need," said Grandma, "are some secrets of your own." She closed the door and we talked about MY Christmas secrets.

I got Mother's button box. Grandma found some thread and pieces of felt. We worked in my room all day.

"What were you two doing all afternoon?" Mother
  asked at dinner.
"Oh, I was just telling Joshua stories about the old
  times," Grandma said. She winked at me.
"And I told her some stories about the new times,"
  I said.

We worked the next day, too.

Grandma showed me how to sew
flowers with colored thread.

She borrowed the wrapping paper and ribbons so no one even guessed it was for MY presents.

While Grandma was helping Mother with dinner,
I made one more secret surprise.

I wrapped it all by myself and hid all my presents underneath the Christmas tree when nobody was looking.

Penny and Abby were giggling. "Oooo, Josh! It's
Christmas Eve!" Penny said. "Just you wait.
Tomorrow there will be surprises for you!"
"Yeah," said Abby. "Tomorrow you get to find out
all the secrets."

"You'll have surprises, too," I said. Grandma
squeezed my hand. I was bursting with my
secrets.

"I know!" squealed Abby. "Oh, I can't wait!
I can't wait!"

On Christmas morning we all opened our packages. I was surprised with a cuddly bunny Mother made for me, the blue mittens and hat with snowmen all around from Grandma, and the tunnel and train station that Daddy made to go with the brand-new train from Santa Claus.

Penny and Abby gave me a bag of marbles for my very own. But I wasn't the only one who had happy surprises.

"Oh, wow! A present from Josh!" Penny exclaimed.
"It's a hair band. Oooo, it's pretty! Did you make
  this, Josh?"
"Look at the button necklace he made for me,"
  Abby said, putting it around her neck.

"So this is what you've been up to," Mother said,
holding up her handkerchief. "Did you really
sew these flowers in the corners? They are
wonderful!"

"So is my picture, Josh," said Daddy. "I'll hang it in
my office."

Grandma liked her special box, too. "I know just
what to keep in this," she said. "All those nice
letters from my grandchildren."

"I guess you can keep a secret," said Abby. "You

kept yours so well that we didn't even know you had any."

Penny laughed. "Maybe next year we'll tell you ours."

"Maybe," said Abby.

"Maybe next year I'll have my own again," I said.

"I like Christmas secrets."